AF291570

HARRIS

ROSA JAMES

authorHOUSE®

AuthorHouse™
1663 Liberty Drive
Bloomington, IN 47403
www.authorhouse.com
Phone: 833-262-8899

Editor: Chanekka Pullens

Published by AuthorHouse 04/08/2021

ISBN: 978-1-6655-2232-8 (sc)
ISBN: 978-1-6655-2231-1 (e)

Print information available on the last page.

DEDICATED TO MY ANGELS IN HEAVEN

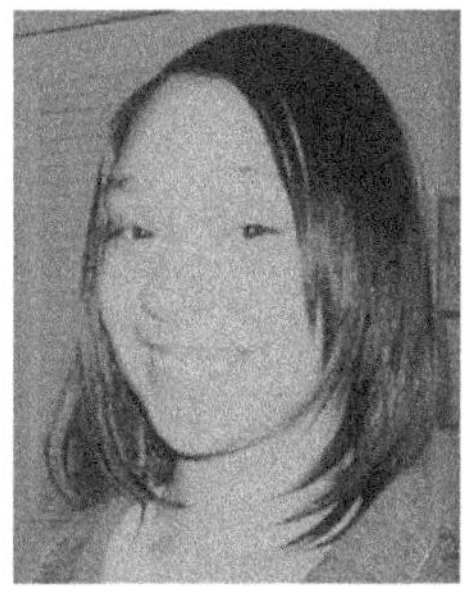

NIA JAMES 2011

PATRICIA JAMES 2018

DENINE MCCORD 2021

CONTENTS

PROLOUGE
JUNE 1, 2019

Waking up every morning has been like a dream. I must pinch myself to make sure this shit is real. I wish I could share this moment with all my niggas, but the journey to this type of happy ending had its casualties.

Rest in peace to my cousin, Reggie, and the homies Tommy and Davis. They were loyal and helped pave the way. Unfortunately, the world could not handle niggas like that, so haters killed them. I still hold their families down because without them, I would have been either in a box or in a cage doing life like my homie Jacob aka Big-slim.

Big-slim was a stone-cold killer. His world was dark. He endured a lot of trauma and seen a lot of fucked up shit. One night Big-slim was high off PCP and killed a police officer at a fast-food restaurant for asking if he was ok. Everyone was shocked on how shit went down. Not me, I knew he was a beast, and he was loyal to me.

After losing four members of my squad, my homie Cameron and I continued to make money and party hard.

Cameron is the closest person to me besides my mother, my younger sister, Shelby, and Uncle Bennie. We are brothers and we break bread with each other. Now, Uncle Bennie is the real goat in the city. He taught me everything I know about the game and is the reason why I hustle so hard.

Having money is all good, but waking up to the love of my life, Twyla, is better. We've been together for two years and it still feels like the first night I seen her at Lenny's. I gave her my number, but she didn't bite at the beginning. Eventually, fate made us run into each other months later at a local pool hall. I used to be a player; now, Twyla has my full attention and quenches the thirst that kept me holding on to multiple women for years.

When I think back, it's hard to believe that I juggled six women for years, only to find one woman that possessed everything I was looking for. Twyla is my rider like Rayvin, she can be submissive like Tameka, she has mad skills in the bedroom like Loretta, her money long like May, she goes with the flow like Toni, and she's nurturing like Daisy. She has me coming home every night and thinking about the little things.

My homie Cameron is not convinced that I am a one-woman man. You would think the twenty-five-carrot ring I placed on Twyla's finger a year ago would confirm it. But I figure once the wedding is over, Cameron would stop doubting me.

As for now, Twyla and I are looking forward to our

wedding in a few days and expanding our family. Since she has no children, one of my biggest priorities is to get her pregnant.

I know my newfound love pisses all my exes off, except for Toni and Rayvin. Toni cares the least. We have a beautiful daughter named Destiny who is 10 years old. Toni was never a mother, so I have taken care of our daughter since she was born. Destiny lives with my son, Harris Jr., and his mother.

Even though Toni does not care about Destiny, she still uses her for stability. I keep a roof over her head, food in her stomach, and drugs in her system. I do this so that she won't use her white girl status in the courts to take my daughter away from me. I know that sounds crazy, but if Toni went into court and put all the shit that I was doing on the table, I believe the judge would have a field day with my black ass.

Now that I think about it, the only times Toni showed any emotion was during sex and when Destiny was born. She seemed to glow at the sight of our daughter, but that light dimmed as soon as she was out of the hospital.

Harris Jr.'s mother, May, is what you call the average independent woman. You know the woman that has everything and don't need anyone. Except when that pussy starts to throb, and the vibrator won't hit the spot. May came from privilege. Her parents are corporate attorneys. She followed in their footsteps becoming a defense attorney.

I remember when she used to be so sweet. She would give her right arm for me. But now, she's bitter. It's my fault because we were starting a family and I broke her heart. We moved into a beautiful home on Ward Parkway, one of the prestigious neighborhoods in Kansas City. Everything was perfect until she started being controlling. To make matters worse, when I was having issues with the property game, she was kicking me when I was down. I left because I was no one's bitch ass nigga and was not tolerating the verbal abuse. Twyla came around that time and took my mind off her. Once May found out about her, the competition was on.

She always thought she was the best woman I ever had. She would laugh at Tameka's infertility, Toni being a deadbeat, Loretta's hoe behavior, Rayvin's loyalty, and Daisy's undying love for me. I did not like how she thought she was better than everyone; and I was glad to see that Twyla shut her down.

While May was trying to be my headache, Loretta was my headache. She was a broke, sack chasing bitch that thought she could fuck her way to the top with me. It's crazy because she was groomed by her mother to hunt for men with money. I am sure the night she was at my uncle's house, she was willing to take any nigga with money. I peeped her thirsty ass from the beginning and had no intentions of dealing with her; but I allowed my lust to take over.

We ended up having a beautiful baby, Karris. So, I had to tolerate Loretta because she was my baby momma. But the bitch could not do shit but fuck! She couldn't cook, she couldn't clean; hell, she could barely make fucking bottles for Karris. I tried to teach her shit, but that bitch just wanted a dick in her mouth all day, every day.

Message to the ladies! Sex has never kept a man forever. As soon as I found a loophole, I walked my ass in a court room and got custody of my daughter. Till this day, Loretta still gives me hell. But not for the fact that I took our daughter, but because I will not give her the dick anymore.

When I think about it, she didn't come to any of the court proceedings. It was easy for me to go in there and lie about how she abandoned our daughter. That I was taking care of Karris all by myself. The judge fell right into that shit. Once I was granted sole custody, I had the best mother in mind and that was Tameka.

You see, Tameka and I relationship was almost as deep as my first love, Daisy. She and I connected during grave circumstances. I always wanted to give Tameka something she was losing, and that was family. My uncle Benny and mother loved Tameka like she was family; but a child was a special love, and I knew she would make a good mother.

My relationship with Tameka taught me how to nurture. She was fragile because life was always taking from her. It began when she lost her father, then her mother. We both shared the tragic loss of losing our son. Majestic died as soon as he was born, and it planted a void in our hearts to lose him. We tried several times to make another child, but after enduring the pain of miscarriages, we realized it wasn't meant to be. In the mist of the drama, I was happy to bring

Karris home to her. Currently, Tameka takes care of Karris as if she carried her in her womb. I'm glad to see her happy.

You know, it was always interesting to watch how these women intimidated each other. For example, out of all the women, Tameka who was the most fragile, was the triple threat to Daisy, who was my first love and baby momma. Daisy and I have three daughters together. A set of twins, Clarise and Daisha who are 14 years old, and our 4-year-old Jamie.

Daisy and I started dating young, so she experienced the little boy growing into a man. I loved her deeply; but she could never heal from all the things I put her through. Because of that, our relationship failed. I wanted to make things work with her, so I tried to be patient and give her space and time to heal.

When she tried to move on with someone else, I could not handle that shit. So, I sabotaged it. I remember my uncle telling me that sometimes we hurt people so much that they do not know how to recover. I damaged Daisy and now I just want her to be happy. I learned that we are better friends and coparents than lovers.

Despite her insecurities, Daisy's personality was always pleasant, and everyone loved her. However, it was something about Tameka that made Daisy unstable. If I had to guess, I would say that Daisy saw the same nurturing being given to Tameka that she received from me, and that fueled her envy. When we had family gatherings, Tameka and Daisy were always present because my family loved them both. I liked how they keep it classy when they were around each other. You would think I had my hands full juggling all these women. But then, there was Rayvin. She was not a baby momma and was the youngest of all the women. Our relationship began because I saw a young woman with potential that needed a role model.

Rayvin became my homie; and our relationship is bonded by loyalty. I molded her into the image I wanted, with a street mind. She was one of my hitters and replaced my homies that was dead or in jail. I trained her to be a stone-cold killer and she has my back until the day I die.

It was fucked up to witness the poor support from Rayvin's own family. She was like the Cinderella and that pissed me off, so I became her family. Later in our relationship we ended up crossing the line and was intimate with each other. Fortunately, that did not shatter Rayvin's loyalty to me. Despite my newfound relationships, Rayvin will always be a rider.

Now, my lady, number seven, Twyla, shines through with all the qualities that can keep me at bay. The whole Kansas City gossip is about me becoming a one-woman man. Some don't believe it, but it's cool. I will let those haters hate because action speaks louder than words.

Well, I am finally home for the night. Man, I can't believe I am coming home at a decent time. Who would have thought I would be tamed? I have a romantic evening planned for my wife to be. I plan to surprise her with dinner; and for dessert, maybe going half on a baby.

My name is Harris and I don't want to be a player anymore.

TONI

Harris used to the hero in my world. But now, the sound of his voice and his touch makes my stomach turn. I dread when things are going bad for him, because that means he's going to take it out on me. I find myself angry at all the other women, resenting whichever one pissed him off because they don't see Harris's wrath.

I know about Tameka, May, Daisy, Rayvin, Loretta, and now, Twyla. There is not much to Harris and me. My role is to cook up his drugs and chill at his spot. I can honestly say that I am the neutral party between Harris and his women. I try to mediate his relationships so that he will not end up taking it out on me.

I am literally his bottom bitch. The Harris that these women are dreaming about and loving, has a lot of deep scars. He is the monster I see. I still cannot believe that I had a daughter with him. Her name is Destiny. I only loved her for one day, the day she was born.

If Harris no longer needs me to cook the drugs, then Destiny would be the leverage I use to maintain food and shelter. I hope I never have to use her as a pawn with her father, because honestly, I don't want the responsibilities of being a mother. But I will do whatever to make sure I get what I need, literally.

I met Harris in 2006 at my ex-boyfriend's trailer home, aka myth lab. My ex would cook up Harris's drugs. He would stick around through the entire process because he didn't trust him. While waiting, Harris and I would chill, play cards, and smoke weed.

Months later, my ex began doing the drugs instead cooking it. That's when he started beating me and skimming off Harris's drugs. I had to think fast to save myself. Either my ex was going to beat me to death, or Harris was going to kill us about his product. Harris needed someone he could trust to cook his drugs and I needed someone to keep a roof over my head, food in my belly, and protection from my ex. So, I revealed to Harris that I knew how to cook the drugs, and that was the beginning of us.

When my ex found out, he was sure I was sleeping with Harris at the beginning. One night, he damn near beat me to death and I had to make a run for it. After living in a battered women's shelter for a week, Harris found me and took me back to his spot.

Moving forward, I cooked Harris drugs and he keep me high, fed, clothed, and a place to live. He even protected me from my crazy ex who kept stalking. The last time I saw him was when Harris caught him lurking in the back yard of the spot. Harris and Rayvin made him get inside the trunk of a car, and I never had an issue again. I knew what happened and was relieved, but I paid for that later. Despite how cool Harris was, he had a dysfunctional side that I don't think anyone knew about.

When Harris was in a dark place, he came to the spot. I remember when we conceived Destiny, it was not pleasant. It was storming that night and I tried to sleep. Harris was in a bad mood, blasting his loud gangster rap. After a couple hours, I managed to dose off. Not for long, because I was awakened by a presence in my bedroom.

I remember Harris was standing over my bed. When I turned on the lamp and looked at him, his eyes were dark. They were dilated because he had taken some pills. When he was like this, I knew what to do. I sat up on the edge of the bed and pulled his sweats down, releasing his manhood. I put him inside my warm mouth and gave him what he needed. He clinched both of his hands around my head and began ramming me. I could barely control my gag reflex. He released minutes later, and in a low voice, he instructed me to get completely naked.

Harris violated every part of me that night. I endured the pain, hoping that it would all end soon. But whatever he had taken gave him stamina for hours. When he was finally finished, he walked naked out of my bedroom and to the bathroom. He ran me some bath water with Epsom salt. When he returned to get me, it was like he transformed from monster back to man again.

I eased out of the bed and walked past him, making my way to the bathroom. I could feel his breath on the back of my neck as I walked slowly, wincing in pain. I submerged myself in the tub, while he sat on the toilet. As I soaked, he talked about all the things that was going on in his life. During that time, he and Tameka lost their son Majestic.

I just listened because I had no words. Shit, my life has been a series of unfortunate events. I could not judge or advise anyone. I was white trash from a trailer park, a product of myth head parents, and endured sexual abuse from my own father. Dysfunction was all I knew and Harris took advantage of that.

I guess you are wondering why I continue to deal with Harris. Well, the answer is simple. I have shelter, food, and drugs. The way I see it is that everything comes with a cost; and if he is not abusing me every moment of the day, then I can handle it.

For entertainment, I sit back and watch all his women. I call them his sidekicks because each of them serves a specific purpose and don't even realize it. They all seem to gravitate to me, except for this new chick, Twyla. At the beginning, I thought it was cute and funny that Twyla had everyone sweating. But then, Cameron told me that my living situation was in jeopardy.

Harris has kicked everyone to the curve. I am not sure what's going on, but he didn't bring me any drugs to cook this week. So, here I am worried that something is wrong, or what Cameron is saying has truth.

Wait, I have a voicemail. Oh, it's Loretta's crazy ass. Maybe she knows something about Harris. Oh, yeah! If her chapter is next, be prepared because that bitch is long winded.

LORETTA

Harris has me twisted if he thinks he is going to keep dodging me, because he knows I can do a lot of damage.

For the past few months, he has been ignoring me. So, I make daily trips through all his known places. Like Tameka's, his slave Toni, that bougie bitch May, and Daisy's gullible ass. I won't lie, I stay clear of his pit-bull Rayvin. I have not been able to get to this new bitch, Twyla. But trust, as soon as I find out where she lives, I am sending a couple bricks through the bitch picture window.

I know I may seem crazy, but Harris fucked me, got me pregnant, and just left me hanging. So, he owes me. I need a brand-new home like May and Daisy because he owes me that. He tried to put me in one of his rental properties, but fuck that! I want the best of the best and I know he can do better. I'm too sexy and my pussy is too good to not be living lovely. He thinks because he took my daughter and gave her to Tameka, that he does not have to pay up.

To make matters worse, I stopped fucking with my friend, Effie, who is now Bennie's wife. If Effie were my real friend, she would have warned me that Harris was taking our daughter. I feel like Harris just used me to get pregnant so that bitch Tameka could have a baby. And for that he owes me, and I want what is due to me. I know it sounds harsh but try and see it from my view.

Harris was so cool when we met at a party his uncle Bennie threw in April 2013. Bennie was a major player in the game and when he threw a party, all the real niggas came out to play. My friend Effie received an invite from Bennie through Facebook and made me her plus one. I was ready to be caught and taken care by a baller, so I was in attendance that night. I made sure I stole an expensive dress from the boutique "TenTwenty5" and made sure everything was done from my lace front bob wig to my freshly pedicured feet.

Bennie was the GOAT of the city so I was excited to finally get a chance to meet him in person. When I arrived at his home that night, he was so fucking fine I had a plan to snatch his ass right from under Effie's nose. But Bennie made it clear that he loved him a dark chocolate woman, so my caramel complexion didn't have a chance. *That was only one fish in the sea*, I thought as threw my pole out again to catch my next fish. At the beginning, I was not feeling pressed because it seemed like every man in the room could be the one, I just needed to catch him.

I spotted Harris, who was chilling at the dining room table preoccupied with the basketball game on the television. I knew a thing about basketball even though I did not care for it. But my mother always told me to be well rounded because it was attractive to men.

I sashayed my thick curvy body over to the dining area, making sure to intentionally block his view with my plump round assets. Harris let out a chuckle as I styled and profiled in front of the television. I was glad he took the bait fast, so I wheeled him in. I took a glimpse at the television to see what teams were playing and the score so that I could spark a conversation that would keep his interest.

When I turned around, I had his full attention. He had a playful expression on his face and it was cute. I returned a sly smile as I made my way to the empty chair next to him and took a seat. We conversed throughout the game, and not long after, we started taking shots and laughing. His uncle came over to join, along with Effie, who had won the battle with many beautiful women in the room.

Hours passed and well past midnight, the guests began to leave. Soon, it was just the four of us playing spades, laughing, and drinking.

Harris and Bennie were the funniest men I had ever met. My stomached ached from laughing as I listened to them go back and forth with each other, telling stories from their past. By 4:00am Bennie and Effie retreated to one of Bennie's five bedrooms, leaving Harris and I alone.

I knew that I was not leaving because Effie was my ride. I anticipated joining Harris in one of the bedrooms and I hoped he felt the same way.

"Well, it looks like your girl staying for breakfast," joked Harris as he stood up and began cleaning off the table.

I sat quietly with my fingers crossed, waiting on an invite. A half hour later, Harris returned from the kitchen looking tired after loading some glasses in the dishwasher.

"I can show you to a bedroom if you want. Bennie is very hospitable, so he has room and honestly, I am too drunk to drive," said Harris, standing over me.

"I will take a bedroom and breakfast. But only if you're cooking," I replied with a flirtatious look, hoping he would join me.

Harris smiled and gestured for me to follow him upstairs. I grabbed my five-inch heels, stood up from the chair, and followed him. The plush carpet seemed to swallow my feet as I walked up the stairs and down the long hall. I had to admit, Bennie's home was decked out with the best of the best. So, I knew his nephew could not be far behind him. The smell of lavender invaded my nose, and the dim lanterns by each door gave the hallway a hotel look.

I was wondering were Effie and Bennie were, but that questioned was answered when we passed one of the doors and I heard the low moans. I was so caught in my thoughts; I didn't realize that Harris stopped at one of the bedroom doors. I bumped into the back of his tall, strapping physique. He turned and laughed before teasing me about being on his hills like his daughters.

Now, I hated to hear he had kids already, but the fact

that he had them on his mind gave me a hint that he was not a deadbeat. Nevertheless, where there are daughters, there are mothers. And so now, I questioned in my mind what chick I had to compete with and was it worth it.

Harris opened the bedroom door and flicked on the light. I was amazed. Bennie's guest room was not just ordinary. It reminded me of a hotel suite, the only thing that was missing was a mint on the pillow.

"You dam right he is very hospitable," I mumbled, walking over to the king size bed, and plopping down on it.

Harris stood in the doorway, nodding in agreement about the comment I made while looking around the room as if he were new to it. Now, the fact that he was not inside the room all over me made me feel a type of way. I knew this fool was not walking away from all of this. So, I had to think fast and bring the big guns out.

"So, where you think you going?" I spoke in a low seductive voice.

Harris stood staring at me for several seconds. His eyes were so dark and hypnotic, I could not read what was on his mind. I allowed my little gold dress to fall to the floor, exposing my pink lace Victoria Secret matching thong and bra. The bra tamed and perked my large breast perfectly. Harris displayed a devious grin. He seemed satisfied with what he seen but he still stood in the doorway.

If he was not going to give me what I wanted, then I was going to get some type of thrill out of it.

I sat back on the bed, spread my legs, and began slipping my index finger in and out my warm wet box. I loved to please myself, so if Harris were not going to take the bait, then at least I would put something on his mind.

My fingers felt so good going in and out, I almost forgot he was standing there. I unsnapped the front buckle on my bra, releasing my big girls with my free hand. I never took my eyes off him as I moaned with great pleasure.

Harris continued to watch. His facial expression was blank, but the fact that he continued to stand there spoke in volumes. I came three times before he finally walked over to the bed. Without warning, he unbuckled his belt and opened his jeans, releasing his dick. It was perfect and my mouth watered at the sight of it. I crawled to the foot of the bed and took him into my mouth. Although not at full attention, he still stuffed it.

Harris's flesh seemed to melt on my tongue. It was like he was massaging the inside of my mouth instead of my tongue massaging him. He began to grow, but I was not worried because I have an awesome gag reflex. I knew I had him when he began to moan and I continued to lick and suck until he exploded down my throat a half hour later. When I backed off, he examined himself and was impressed that there was no mess.

My mother told me that sucking dick would get you the house on the hill if done with perfection. Harris slipped himself back into his clothing and fastened his belt. He then informed me that breakfast would be served at 11:00am, before leaving me alone in the bedroom.

Now there I was sitting half naked on the bed waiting for Harris to return the favor. You would think that after using one of my winning moves, he would at least cuddle with a bitch. He left me in the bedroom with a wet pussy. At this point it was clear that he was giving me a chase and I had more tricks up my sleeve.

I went into the private bathroom where there individually wrapped toothbrushes and mini toothpaste in a basket along the sink. Once again, Bennie was going out of his way to spoil his guest. I remember thinking that my girl Effie better make sure she keeps him happy or I would find a way to get him. I brushed my teeth and showered before laying in the bed naked, hoping that Harris would return, but I fell asleep.

Later that morning, I was awakened by the aroma of breakfast. I hurried out of bed, brushed my teeth, and slipped into my dress. I did not bother to put my panties or heels on before going downstairs to the kitchen where Harris was standing over the stove cooking. He was wearing a tank top, grey sweats, and house shoes. I could tell his dick was swinging free and I imagined him bending me over the kitchen table.

I needed to know more about this man, so I started asking questions. I learned that Bennie's house was Harris's home away from home. He would not go into detail about where he lived, so I assumed it was a bitch in the picture that he was halfway shacking up with. I questioned how he made a living and hit another dead end when he responded that he had various avenues of income. At that point, Harris was sending all the red flags, but I wanted to confirm my intuition so I would stay in the race.

Our conversation was interrupted by Bennie and Effie entering the kitchen, they were both glowing. I felt a bit envious but reminded myself that I was going to win with Harris. I had to be patient and look beyond his flags.

We all sat, ate breakfast, and talked about some of the weird guest that attended the party the night before. After eating, Effie and I went on our way. But not before I locked my number in Harris's phone.

Three weeks passed, and can you believe that I did not hear from Harris at all. Effie and Bennie were moving fast and damn near exclusive. I was too embarrassed to tell her what really happened between Harris and I that night. However, I wondered if she knew because she was basically living with Bennie. They were hosting a party Memorial Day weekend. Effie sent me an invite by text and I made sure I would be there so that I could run into Harris and see what was up.

On the day of the party, I dressed to impress, wearing a navy-blue maxi-dress that hugged my curves. Effie picked me up and I helped her set things up while Bennie grilled. And that's when I got the true smack in the face. Harris had a whole bitch living in Bennie's house named Tameka. The site of Effie and Tameka walking around like they owned the place irritated me, but I played it cool. I planned to stick around and observe Harris, while looking for a new nigga.

Tameka was fine, darker than me, and her hair was thick, long, and straight falling past her mid back. She was tall and considered a full-figured woman, but her small waist complimented her bodacious curves. Tameka was giving me a shapelier Remy Ma vibe and I could see why Harris had her put up.

After hanging out for a while, Harris finally made an appearance. He did not ignore me and made sure I was comfortable in a friendly 'you did not suck my dick three weeks ago' manner. It made me feel some type of way, so I was distracted myself with another man trying to get up on me.

Now I said that I would look out for other niggas, but Harris was all in my head and I wanted him by any means. I played along with another man to see if I would catch Harris's attention. Epic fail! Because Harris was not paying me any attention especially when Tameka was in the room. He was very attentive to her as she sat on his lap laughing and talking to people.

Hours later, I was relieved when she retreated to one of the bedrooms upstairs and never returned. At that point, Harris continued to enjoy himself playing dominoes with some of his cousins from out of town. The guy that was trying to holla at me started pursuing another chick, but I didn't care because he didn't help me get Harris attention anyway.

Suddenly, a woman came through the front door. She was caramel complexion like me, but tall and shaped exactly like Tameka. She wore long bundles of weave and her makeup was flawless. When she walked past me her perfume lingered into my nostrils, it smelled amazing and expensive.

The woman smiled and greeted everyone in the room. I knew from the moment she walked in she belonged to Harris and I was right, it was his baby momma Daisy. Their twin daughters, Clarise and Daisha, came running in. They hugged Bennie and various other family members. I learned there was a third child name Jamie that was the youngest. She was at the house the whole time napping when I arrived. I assumed Jamie was upstairs with Tameka throughout the day, that's why she did not hangout that long.

Daisy hugged Bennie and they joked for a while before she joined Harris and the girls at the table in the dining room. I decided to join Effie in the kitchen. She was assisting Bennie's sister, who I learned was Harris's mother Cassandra. His mother was nice, but you could tell that life had been hard by the battle scars on her face.

Effie made me another drink and we sat on the back patio. She caught me up on her new life with Bennie. I found out she had already moved in with him and they had plans on having a baby. It was perfect because Effie did not have any children, along with Bennie. But I felt envious that she struck the jackpot, while I was still being teased by Harris.

Suddenly, Daisy came to the back patio and joined us. We all sat and conversated about things from the latest reality shows to the best hair stylist in the city. That was before Harris's daughters came out disturbing us.

Daisy was very attentive to her girls. You could tell the youngest daughter, Jamie, was spoiled rotten because she demanded her mother's undivided attention. I remember Harris came outside multiple times to get Jamie in attempts to give her mother a break.

I loved watching Harris be a dad to his daughters. He was kind and gentle and seemed to know what he was doing.

I fantasized being his baby momma and sharing a spoiled daughter with him. But why was I kidding myself, I didn't really want a kid unless the baby daddy was going to spoil me.

Suddenly, the smell of weed invaded my nose. When I looked up, Tameka and Harris's mother was sitting on the upper balcony smoking weed.

Now, I knew for sure that Harris was not for the taken. Sure, Bennie was hospitable, but Tameka was at home and comfortable. At that point, I was confused and ready to call it a day. I went back inside to see if there were any other eligible bachelors for the taken.

I enjoyed myself for the remainder of the night but had no luck with bagging a baller. All the men in Harris family were quite charming, and with that came the women coming to claim their men. With no luck, a couple hours later, I called an Uber.

I slipped outside in the darkness and watched the map, the driver would arrive in ten minutes. I was over it all and ready to go home and get some rest. The large oak tree in Bennie's yard concealed my head that poked slightly above the retainer wall at the beginning of the yard, so no one would see me.

To my luck, Daisy, Harris, and the girls came outside. He walked them to the car and gave everyone a kiss, including Daisy. He backed away from the car, waving as Daisy steered her black Range Rover away. I remembered thinking he must make sure they live good as I watched the Rover go down the street and make a left turn.

Suddenly, Harris turned around and addressed me as if he knew I was standing here all along. His eyes were dark and hypnotic as he questioned my presence outside. When I told him that my uber would be arriving soon, the disgusted look on his face let it be known he did not like the idea. He snatched the phone out of my hand and cancelled it before reaching in his pocket and pulling out his keys.

As we made our way to his Cadillac SUV, I remember him reprimanding me. "You are tripping, Loretta. The men in this family don't tolerate women leaving in cabs and shit.

You better be glad Bennie didn't catch you because he would curse you out," he finished while opening the passenger door and helping me inside.

He shut the door and hurried to the driver side. Once inside, he started the engine and we drove away.

"So, you live in the projects?" Harris questioned, breaking the silence.

I wondered how he knew, then realized that Effie must be running her mouth. Embarrassed, I gave him a long explanation about being in between places due to the fire and had to move into the projects with my mother.

Harris gave a nod as he continued to focus on the road. I was relieved that he did not seem to be judgmental. I figured this was GOD giving me another chance and I decided to play dirty at this point. It was either now or never with this man. I refused to return to Bennie's and watch Harris flaunt his women around, because I was going to be his woman.

Harris parked in front of my mother's unit. Although it appeared my mother was not home, I was too ashamed to invite him inside. I remember feeling like a failure as I looked at my mother's front door from the parking lot. My mother talked all that shit about catching ballers and none of her niggas got her out the hood. She was only riding around in nice cars, eating good, dressing nice, and getting help for delinquent bills here and there. Fuck that shit! I was looking for a nigga that would save me and get me the fuck out of the projects for good.

Harris cracked the windows and fired up a blunt before reaching in his console and pulling out a fifth of Remy Martin. We sat, smoked, and took shots of the Remy while talking. I learned a lot about him in that couple hours. His family originated from the very projects I was dreading to come home to.

Harris amused me as he pointed out areas where some of his unforgettable moments happened. He also shared a sad story of his little cousin, Reggie, being shot in the head right behind the very unit I lived in. I learned that Harris's came from a family of hustlers and it started with his grandfather, Alex, who was murdered in the nineties.

I shared some of my stories and, thanks to the liquor, I revealed some of my weaknesses and struggles. Harris surprised me being a great listener and giving valuable input. Just listening to his encouraging words validated why I was attracted to him. Tameka was going to have to watch out because a new sheriff was in town.

Without warning, I straddled him. My plump ass could barely fit between him and the steering wheel. I stuck my tongue into his mouth and French kissed him passionately, hoping I could pry through this solid exterior and make him mines. He did not resist as he let his seat back as far as it could go.

He closed his eyes and began savoring my large nipples, going back and forth from right to left, giving both equal pleasures. I unbuckled his belt and unfastened his jeans, releasing the beautiful dick I took in my mouth almost a month ago. I ripped my panties off and slid down, allowing him to fill me up.

I wanted to scream, but I had to keep it together to let him know I was a big girl and could handle him. He opened his eyes, seemingly surprised that I was sitting on an ocean. You could see the lust in his eyes as I gently went up and down on him, forcing soft low moans out of his mouth. He sat back, relaxed, and let me do it all. I had no objection because he would repay me later.

The open sunroof prevented the presidential tinted windows from fogging and I was thankful for that. I rode his dick while passionately kissing him until he exploded inside of me.

Satisfied, I smiled and gave him a kiss on the lips. We caught our breath. Suddenly, his phone started to vibrate. I returned to the passenger seat while the female voice continued to yell in his ear. I wonder if it was Tameka realizing her man was gone and the mysterious girl that sat on the couch was missing also.

Just as I suspected, it was Tameka and based on his responses, she thought he left with Daisy. If Tameka was worried about her, then I needed to be focused on her as well.

I gave Harris another kiss before getting out the truck, leaving him to his call. If all goes well, I would be the next woman that intimidated Tameka sooner than later.

Months later, just as I predicted I became the woman that intimidated Tameka in my second trimester of pregnancy. When Harris found out I was carrying his baby, he waited on me hand and foot and never missed a doctor's appointment.

I was sure I had him, and we would evolve. But I soon learned that it was really all about the baby and our relationship would never get off the ground.

I did not want to just be a baby momma. I wanted to be wifey in the big house like Effie, who was pregnant with Bennie's baby. We were due around the same time and I anticipated our babies growing up together.

Harris was not spending a lot of time at Bennie's because I was occupying his time. He would pick me up, take me to his spot, and I would chill with him and this chick named Toni for hours. He never took me to Bennie's and I knew it was because Tameka was still there.

When I was too big to have sex, he stopped picking me up except for doctor's appointments. I wasn't tripping though because I was too lazy to be running the streets with him. However, I needed transportation for errands, so I began to complain because it was time for him to start paying up. He listened to my grievance and brought me some type of average midsize car. It was not a Range like Daisy's or Tahoe decked out with rims like Tameka. It was a simple car that got me where I needed to go. Now that I had a car I only saw Harris at the doctor appointments.

He gave me a debit card that he loaded weekly for food and other essential things.

I spent my nights driving around, stalking every location I knew he would be at. One night, I was sitting down the block from Bennie's to see if I would see Harris. I ended up falling asleep in the car. Hours later, I was awakened by Harris tapping on the window and he was pissed. As a result, he took the car and moved me in one of his raggedy rental houses. That kept me content until I gave birth to our daughter.

He kind of moved in after Karris was born. I was happy he was spending time with us despite the fact his full attention was on the baby. He even slept on the day bed in the nursery. At first, I argued with him a lot about not paying me any attention. But after a while, I gave in and went with the flow. As our daughter got older, Harris reframed from spending five nights a week to maybe one night a week and gave me the car back.

I guess he thought that I would not be able to stalk him with a whole baby to drag along. But I got clever and moved my cousin Maria in with me. Everyone thought Maria and I were sisters because we were raised together. With Maria at home with Karris, I was able to stalk Harris to see what he was up too.

I learned that he was spending nights at Daisy's when he was not at the spot. They were even doing family things together. That meant that there had to be trouble in paradise with Tameka. But it took the cake when I found out that Harris and Toni had a daughter named Destiny; and to make matters worse, Destiny was living with a chick named May who was the mother of his only living son Harris Jr.

I was so overwhelmed with all the new information, I wanted to ring Harris fucking neck. Then things got messy when I got an unexpected visitor. The site of Tameka through the peep hole made my stomach knot up.

Maria was not home, and when I opened that door Tameka beat my ass until she was ready to stop. I did not bother to call Harris because he was not answering my calls anyway. But Tameka did and told him everything. The next morning, I was awakened by Harris.

The benefit of getting my ass beat was that Harris was more compassionate with me. He dabbed witch hazel on my black eye daily and allowed me to rest while he took care of Karris. Things seemed to start going in my favor, then boom, I found out that Harris was fucking Maria while I was out pretending to look for a job. I remember back tracking that day and found them fucking on the kitchen floor while Karris slept peacefully in her baby bed.

I snapped and Maria ran out the house naked. She hopped into Harris's truck and they fled the scene; but not before I sent a brick through his back window. An hour later, my mother called me to inform me that Harris dropped Maria off at her place. Maria told my mother everything and she tried to apologize to me. I accepted her apology because she was family, but things would never be the same between us.

Moving forward, Harris kept his distance. He only kept the bills paid at the house and visited Karris consistently once per week. Then, he started picking her up and keeping her for days, so I began to make that difficult. I started with changing the locks so that he would not just come in when he wanted. Yeah, I was jealous and still am of the love he gives Karris. I know that's his seed, but I wanted Harris to love and take care of me. It was time for him to compensate me for the damages like carrying a baby for nine months.

I was going to use Karris as collateral because I needed to live lavish like Daisy and Harris was going to be the provider. So, one day when he was on his visit, I let him know what I expected. He sat and listened while Karris played with his cell phone. He had an ornery look on his face and found my words amusing. I made it clear that if my needs were not met, then I would cause problems.

Once I finished stating my demands, Harris let me have it. Can you believe he told me to get a job? When I compared my situation to Daisy's, he smirked and replied that Daisy didn't just sit on her ass. I spat, "yeah right", and began talking about Tameka. Harris laughed and told me to focus on myself and stop sizing myself up to other women because it made me look pathetic.

His words hurt me to the core because he was right. I was comparing myself to other bitches instead of finding myself. As days went by, I fell into a deep depression. I sat in the house and took care of my daughter while he kept the bills paid. Hell, I even started letting Daisy come pick up Karris so she could spend time with her sisters. I remember Daisy never seemed to be stressed or bothered. She was always smiling and pleasant. Her happiness irritated me and I could not grasp how she and Toni could just be so chill with a nigga like Harris.

My depression was taking a toll on me and my solid body was slimming. Drinking became my favorite past time. The deeper I fell the longer Karris was staying away from me and I didn't even fight it. Soon, a letter came into the mail from the Kansas City Family Court. I damn near lost myself when I read it. Harris was granted sole custody of Karris. After reading the document, I began going through the other mail that was piled up in a bin under the mail slot. I found that I missed three court dates. I felt dumb. Harris was playing all along and now he had Karris. I had nothing to manipulate him with.

Soon, the utilities started becoming disconnected. Eventually, I just woke up one day and went home to my mother's, leaving the front door to his house wide open. I stayed inside for several months trying to process what just happened and how I allowed myself to lose a game that I started. I honestly underestimated Harris because the only thing he was falling for was Karris.

When I started to rise from the darkness, it was time to catch up with my good friend Effie. We had a three-hour conversation on the phone, and I found out that my baby girl was being mothered by Tameka. What made it more fucked up is that Effie had no idea that Karris was my baby. After that conversation I never heard from Effie again.

My sadness turned to rage, and I wanted Harris to feel my wrath. That is why I am the baby mother from hell till this day. I burned down the rental property he tried to put me in. His baby momma, May, has a restraining order on me; and Daisy has pulled a gun on me.

Things at home with my mother are tense. She does not allow a day to go by without expressing the disgust she has because I let my daughter go. Honestly, if I cannot get the full package, then at least my daughter can get a taste of the good life. I didn't want children anyway unless it was to please a man that was going to take care of me. These days I am just making Harris life miserable and dodging the authorities.

I make regular drive by to his spot, vandalize his houses and cars, stalk his baby mommas, and try to get at him whenever I see him. Yeah, it is a lonely life, but Harris is going to feel my rage.

Now, he has this new woman, Twyla. They are supposed to get married in a few days. However, the other day I got an unexpected visit from Rayvin. She is who I refer to as Harris's pit bull. She is concerned about his whereabouts. I just told her that he is probably hiding at his uncle Bennie's house under that bitch Tameka.

TAMEKA

These days, I wish that me and that crazy bitch Loretta was cordial enough to discuss Harris. I am sure her stalking ass knows everything. One thing about Loretta is that she talks to damn much and I am sure her chapter was longer than everyone's.

Things have not been great in over a year between Harris and I. But I am fortunate to have a wonderful daughter, Karris, who is now 5 years old. I still reside at his uncle Bennie's house and Effie and I have become best friends. They are my family no matter what happens between Harris and me. Let me start from the beginning.

I relocated from North Carolina to Kansas City, Missouri after my father died. I graduated with my engineering degree and reunited with my mother, Tammy, who was the only relative I had left.

I moved in with her and started a great career at General Motors. My mother was a drug addict and alcoholic, so it was nothing to come home and find her passed out. A year later she was diagnosed with HIV.

Learning that time was running out, I saved my money

so I could purchase a home so she could spend her last days in a nice place instead of the projects. When I was ready to purchase it, my mother wanted to stay in the projects.

Within a couple of years, her virus advanced to AIDS. The last year of her life I had to take leave from work to take care of her.

That is when I met Harris. He knew my mother from the streets, and they were cool with each other. He would come and check on her from time to time. When she was having good days, they would sit on the front porch and converse for hours. I never paid Harris any mind and stayed in my bedroom until my mother called me. I didn't want to disturb her company. As the virus progressed it got rough because my mother needed advanced care around the clock. Some nights it felt like she was not going to make it and I had no one around to support me emotionally.

One night, I sat on the porch crying as I came to terms with her fate. Harris surfaced out the blue with a twelve pack and a couple joints, expecting to chill with my mother. When he saw me crying, he knew that was out the question.

Harris sat with me and I gave him an update. He hugged, said that things would be okay, and that I was not alone anymore. From that night until my mother died, he spent every single night with us being the support I needed.

I had to admit those couple of months were the best and worst time for me. My mother was dying, and Harris and I grew closer. My mother really liked him. I remember on her death bed she asked Harris to look out for me because I would have no one once she was gone. She also told him that she wished that I had given her a couple grandbabies to spoil before she died.

Harris and my mother were good friends and I could not believe that he was her dealer in the past. His feelings for my mother were genuine. Bennie was cool as well, he came down from time to time to visit my mother before she took her last breath.

My mother died on a Wednesday morning and Harris was by her side when she died. After arranging for her body to be picked up, I did not hesitate to call movers. I had been packing for the past few months anticipating this day. I knew once my mother took her last breath, I was not spending another night in that apartment.

When Harris learned I was checking in a hotel, he disagreed and took me to Bennie's house.

Bennie was very welcoming and almost too generous. I thought they wanted something in return and was prepared to pay money, but that was not the case. Bennie became the uncle I never had. He did not allow me to isolate myself while I grieved.

On the day of my mother's services, I didn't expect anyone but Bennie and Harris to help me send her off. But to my surprise, the home health nurses attended, and Harris showed up with his mother, Cassandra, his sister, Shelby, and a few other relatives.

I was also grateful to experience complete strangers love me just as much as my parents did. Everyone was genuine. I learned that Cassandra and my mother was close when they ran the streets together. When she told me some of the stories about the things she and my mother used to get into, I understood why my mother left me with my father.

Despite my mother's lifestyle, my father would never talk bad about her. So, he would repeat the good stories from the first year of my life, before she left us. That is the reason why I was able to find her and build a relationship, instead of holding resentment.

Now, with Harris and his family, I began to move on and heal. Of course, he and I grew closer. Our relationship is not perfect, but I owe so much to that man because he nurtured me mentally. For that he will always be my family.

Months after my mother was buried, Harris and I became intimate. It was just one of those nights, we connected and made love. From that night on, we had a unique relationship and was not exclusive. Only the people that came around Bennie's really knew about us because I stayed close to home.

On my 21st birthday, Harris was determined to get me out of the house. He set up a romantic trip to Miami. It was my first time going and I was excited because we had a beach house. We did a few activities and relaxed. On the beach one night, Harris said he wanted to give me something special that I did not have and would complete me.

I conceived Majestic on the beach that night. When we returned to Kansas City, Harris spoiled me for the next nine months, along with Bennie, and Cassandra.

Now don't get me wrong, our life was not a fairytale. Harris was still doing his dirt, but I choose not to pay any attention to that because he was satisfying me mentally and physically. I was looking forward to my son and enjoying watching Harris be a father. He was so happy sometimes I had to make him leave to give me some space.

Then I went into labor and gave birth. Our son died an hour later. Once again, I was saying goodbye to something that was a part of me.

Bennie was not getting me out this room easy this time. I fell into a deep depression. Our son would have been the original Harris Jr. But since he was deceased, we decided to name him Majestic in hopes for a Harris Jr. later. That's one reason why I can't stand May's bougie ass to this very day; she has his first living son.

Harris and I tried to make another child, but after several miscarriages, the doctor removed my ovaries and told me it was a done deal. It took me a long time to come to terms with the fact that once I was gone, my family's bloodline would be extinct. It also bothered Harris a lot that I was the last living individual in my family. I remember him saying that he never knew anyone that had absolutely no one. He used to have me go on all those ancestral sites in hopes there was somcone out there that I didn't know about.

I felt worthless. What was my purpose on earth if I could not bear children? I was insecure and felt like Harris could do what he wanted because I could not give him a child. So, I separated myself from the world. I spend my days only working and staying at home in the bedroom.

I was slowly pushing Harris away by the day. Things really got tense when I stopped having sex with him. This really bothered him, and he sometimes became frustrated and insisted on having sex. He would always catch me in the shower. He would hold me, stroke me, and whisper that it would be okay. The words felt good at that moment, but deep down I knew it would not. I could not have a child and my family legacy would no longer exist once I died.

When Harris Jr. arrived, May was barely two days out of the hospital when she popped up at Bennie's with her newborn baby. I felt like jumping off a bridge when I saw that beautiful baby boy. If you are wondering how I was able to be in the same room as May and Harris Jr. without losing my cool, well it was simple. My fucked-up head allowed me to tolerate a lot of bull crap that Harris had going on. Trust me when your mind is not healthy, the decisions you make are distorted and unhealthy.

I came to terms that sex would be the only thing that would make me feel like a woman. I started willingly giving it up to Harris again and used the intimacy to feel again. I was so numb and that was the only moment I felt my feelings were real. Then, five years ago Harris brought me

Karris. It's crazy because when I first found out about the baby, I made a visit to Loretta and beat her ass. Now I regret that because Loretta blessed me with a beautiful daughter and something to live for.

When he brought me Karris, he said he loved me and regretted not being able to give me a child naturally. He said this was the gift that he was determined to give me. He felt that God made a mistake not allowing me to have children naturally.

At that moment, I fell back in love with him. While I was allowing myself to die, Harris was fighting for me. He loves all of me flaws and all, and he was all about family. No woman could never take away what we have, whether it is a bit distorted or not.

Unfortunately, Harris and I would be family, but never complete our own. I was ready to move from Bennie's house and live happily ever after. But over the last couple of years, Harris has been preoccupied with someone else. He barely comes and stays with me. I also learned that he had a loft downtown that I never stepped foot in. But I can't dwell on that mess because he blessed me with Karris, and we co-parent very well. We went to court and he gave me joint custody, and he wants me to adopt her to carry on my family name. That's all I want to care about.

Effie recently told me about the wedding in a few days. Harris usually comes and visits Karris once per week or at least calls her every other day. But I have not heard from him in the past week, and I am more worried if he is okay. Even the bitch May has popped up at Bennie's, looking for Harris. I have been calling his phone and now it is just going straight to voicemail. This is not like Harris; especially when it comes to his children.

MAY

Now, where the hell is Harris? I just stopped by the last place he could be and that's Bennie's. He was supposed to take our son to be fitted for his tuxedo for this wedding.

If you are wondering, I am May, the best woman that Harris ever had. Our son is 10 years old, Harris Jr., who everyone calls Junior. He is the apple of my eye and keeps me sane through all the madness his father put me through. Junior is the pleasant reminder of the good things I shared with his father. If it were not for him, I probably would have jumped off a bridge over a year ago when I found out his father broke my heart and wasted my time.

It is crazy that despite the pain I felt with Harris, I still find myself yearning for him when my world is at a standstill. I must keep myself busy to stay sane, because nothing in the companionship or intimacy department means anything if I do not share it with Harris.

I am amazed that a woman like myself, so smart and successful, could get caught in the Harris's web of heartache. My law degree has afforded me great opportunities and a good life. In everyone's eyes, I am this powerful woman that you could lean on mentally, financially, and physically. But even the strong break down and being in love makes you delusional.

I still have not shared with my family, or even my close friend, Sybil, the dynamics of the relationship between Harris and me. I am so embarrassed. Coming from a prestigious family, they would shun me for being so weak and falling for a street nigga like Harris.

I wouldn't say that Harris was out for my money because he had his own. But I felt that he was attracted to my financial stability. Every woman he had, needed him financially, except for myself. Hell, he was still on my cell phone family plan up until the last year when he and this Twyla went exclusive.

I remember when he started talking to her. I would screen the text messages and how many times they spoke on a daily. The person in those text messages was the same charming man that I had experienced at the beginning of our relationship. It was clear Harris was the pursuer in their relationship and he was consistent with her. He and Twyla were heading for longevity. Before I knew it, he returned the cell phone to me by mail.

At that moment, I knew he was moving on. I sometimes sit and hope that he would use his key and walk through the front door, but that never happens. I try to process the failed relationship, and hope that I would be able to allow someone else in my heart sooner than later. But I admit, I am still trying to flush him out of my system.

I remember meeting Harris when he and his friend, Jacob aka Big-Slim, walked into my firm on a hot July day ten years ago. Big-Slim needed legal representation and Harris was there for financial support. That's the first thing that attracted me to him besides his deep dark eyes. I could not stop making eye contact with him during the consultation.

I remember Big-Slim becoming a bit agitated with our flirting. But I understood, he was facing some serious charges and was in desperate need of help to avoid the death penalty. I regained my focus to the matter at hand, confident that Harris was not leaving my office without making sure we kept in contact with each other. Moreover, by the end of the meeting, Harris paid me a retainer and invited me to dinner that very night.

Usually, I waited at least a week before seeing a man after we exchanged numbers. I never knew why. It was just what I always seen and done without questioning it. But who could decline an invite from a man handing you $10,000.00 in cash? Even if I was not interested in Harris, I still felt obligated to attend at least one dinner date.

That evening, I left the office, hurried to my loft less than a mile from the office, and prepared for my date. I didn't know where Harris was taking me, so I aimed for comfortable with a hint of sexy. I selected a thin black knit, easy access, all-purpose dress that hugged my petite curves and exposed my wonderful shoulders. The dress stopped just a couple inches above my knees, and I wore some black heels that tied around my well-toned calves. I let my long natural sixteen-inch hair drape down so it could flow with the wind. My makeup was light, giving him the natural me, and just for the thrill, I wore no panties.

We met back at my office a couple hours later. I sat on the bench outside my building, enjoying the warm night air. When Harris's drop top black Camaro entered the parking lot and parked next to my Lexus, the hum of his hemi engine made me throb; but I kept my composure. It was not like me to be turned on by bad boys and fast cars. I knew I was going to lose my mind fast with this man. But I ignored the warning as I hopped in the passenger side of his car.

At the beginning of the ride, we were both silent allowing B-Legit's "Check it out" to echo through his sound system as we rode. The warm air feathered through my silky freshly pressed hair. I knew it turned him on, so I continued to look to my right so he could get a full look over of me.

After the song ended and the radio spokesman began to talk, we started to converse. Harris made me feel comfortable. He was funny and entertaining. I could not stop laughing. But my laughter came to a halt when we parked in front of a house on the northeast side of town. I looked around mortified that we were in the middle of an impoverished ghetto. The perplexed look on my face was a dead giveaway that I was not use to this type of environment.

Harris smirked and exited the car, leaving me with my thoughts. As he entered the small ranch style house, I remember thinking how he had me all messed up. I knew already that this night would be our one and only. Wishing I wore panties now, I just continued to focus on my surroundings, not wanting to be robbed or anything.

Minutes later, Harris exited the house. I noticed a white girl standing in the rod iron door. I searched her face for a sign of who she was, her emotionless gaze seemed unthreatening. I turned away and focused on Harris entering the car. With no explanation, he turned on the engine and sped away unbothered.

We made our way to the Plaza were Harris made reservations at my favorite restaurant. After the valet took his car, we went inside. I ordered a Hawaiian steak with vegetables and a potato. Harris ordered the same. He said it was his favorite and that was the first thing I learned that we had in common.

Our conversation was more detailed during dinner. We talked about everything from politics to the issues in our community. After we ate, we walked around the Entertainment District and talked more.

I learned that Harris was about the street life, of course, but he was smart and had plans to be bigger. I admired that. He told me he had two daughters and that he was not with the mother. I sighed in relief because these days it was normal for men to have a baby mother on a string while casually dating.

Time seemed to fly that night, and before you knew it was 1:00am. I was glad I had court late the next day so I could sleep in. The walk to the car consisted of flirting. Harris was loving my long hair and athletic body. He said I reminded him of Jada Pinkett-Smith.

The liquor was doing its job of making us more relaxed with each other. I remember my love-box was wet and throbbing. I was on ten with this man and this was not normal for me. I quickly recanted my regrets for not wearing any underwear as we entered the car.

Harris did not rush to start the car once inside. Instead, he searched his console, pulled out a joint, and fired it up before looking at me with a devious look. Once I smiled, he started the engine, then drove away. He took me to the lake where we chilled, talked, and smoked.

I felt like I would explode. I just wanted him to have his way with me. I took a puff of his joint so I could relax while we talked more. Once the joint was gone, he threw the doobie out the window, sat sideways, then focused on me. We took several minutes just looking at each other. His hair was cut low and his line was flawless. His eyes were dark and hypnotic, complimenting his bronze complexion. He had no facial hair but was not a pretty boy. His look was simple but sexy. When he smiled, the diamonds that covered his front teeth glistened. He had no piercings or tattoos and his strapping country boy physic was turning me on by the second. I imagined him lifting me up and just fucking me in the middle of the parking lot.

Suddenly, we began to kiss. I remember thinking, "Damn! I am not a good kisser." But for some reason, my lips and tongue were like "Wee Wee" with Harris. He slipped his hands up my dress. It turned me on more to know he was going to get a big surprise. When he found that I was commando, the gentle growl from him was assurance that I had turned him on. His reaction made my juices drip as he massaged me with his middle finger, going in and out of me slowly.

Harris was so good with his hands, I remember thinking, "Damn, I do not need the full experience. He could have just kissed and touched me all night!" Then, he stopped and started the engine.

He drove onto Highway 71 and resumed finger fucking me. It felt so good, I did not care that the top was down. I needed Harris and did not care where he was taking me. I damn near broke his belt buckle to get his jeans open. I spit before wrapping my lips around his manhood. I could not believe he was not at full attention after all the making out. This let me know he had control and that it was going to be a long night.

I felt him growing in my mouth, and at full attention, I had to let up. He drove and rubbed his fingers through my hair while I pleased him. I was so into it, that I did not realize we parked at his place until he gently pulled my head up. I looked around, trying to regain my surroundings as he buckled his pants and exited the car.

He opened my door, allowing me to exit. I was dizzy in a good way. He smacked my ass gently before closing the car door and leading the way. I had no idea where I was at all. But I did not care because I felt secure with Harris and was more than eager to continue this adventure. On the elevator, we wasted no time continuing were we left off. He kissed me passionately and massaged my body. My dress was up, exposing it all and I did not care.

Once the elevator stopped, we exited into his lavish loft. I took time to look around for any signs of a woman to ensure this was a bachelor's pad. His place was cozy and had a lot of high-end furniture. I loved a man that liked the finer things.

I took a seat on the white leather couch, being careful to tuck my dress. I didn't want my juices to spill on his couch.

Harris was rolling another joint while talking on the phone. His back was turned to me and I could not make out the words, but I could tell that the conversation was tense.

I wondered if it was a woman looking for her man. And if so, I did not care at this point because he had to finish what he started. After ending the call, he tossed the phone on the counter and grabbed a lighter before joining me on the couch. I stole the joint from his hands and took a puff.

Feeling myself, I stood up in front of him and took my dress off, revealing my naked body. When I kneeled to untie my heels, he stopped me, and whispered to keep them on. He scooted to the edge of the couch, before taking in one of my C-cup breasts. My eyes rolled in the back of my head and I wondered who the hell taught him how to do this. His hands were gentle, and his tongue massaged my body. I was in the zone and don't remember how I ended up on his soft white rug.

He eased inside of me and began stroking me with precision. His facial expression was so sexy and intense as he took every part of me; like I was the best thing he had ever had. Just when you think you had good or even great, here comes Harris with amazing sex. I will warn you that once you have him. you may not find anyone else that will top him.

Until this day, I have not found another man that could make me feel like that. The chemistry and sex were always the best, even when we were on bad terms. Of course, if you were reading every detail, you would notice that one key factor was not a part of our first night. A condom. Nine months later, Junior was here weighing eight pounds even.

Those are the two things I do not regret about Harris. The sex and our son. But everything else was pure uncut betrayal and pain. After that night, we had good days, but the bad days began to outweigh the good fast.

The white girl that was in the front door that night,

I found out before Junior entered the world, that her role was validated. Her name was Toni, and she was carrying his daughter, Destiny, who was born a few months before Junior. I was depressed about the information and for the remainder of my pregnancy, Harris did all he could to lift my spirits. When Junior was born, it brought us closer, but only for a little while.

I didn't want to lose him, so I overextended myself to secure our relationship. He had money, but I offered mine and he took it with no hesitation. You see, street niggas need to see a sacrifice to trust. So, I showed Harris that I was willing to do anything for him and was not checking for what he had.

But no matter what I did, it seemed like there was always a wall; even after learning that Toni was not a serious threat. Harris was not consistent, even when we were supposed to be living together. Soon, Destiny moved with me. We co-parented and split the bills, but he still was seldomly seen.

My mother would always say, "What lies in the dark comes to the light." My loving sister, god rest her soul, would say, "Don't go digging because you will find what you don't want to see."

So, I took both of those sayings and used it to balance my way throughout the roller coaster ride Harris had me on. I learned a lot about his relationship with his daughter's mother, Daisy. He introduced us after Junior was born. She didn't seem threatened or upset that I was now labeled as his woman. Daisy's reaction made me secure that she was not the baby momma on the string. The twins would come over and spend time with Destiny and Junior all the time.

However, overtime my intuition kicked in and I began to feel threatened by Daisy. I overheard Clarise and Daisha talking about Harris and Daisy spending time together. Then, I noticed that Daisy was always coming to the rescue when Harris and I argued. They were chilling like homies, while I was at home with all the children. Whenever I questioned Harris about it, he would get extremely frustrated with the conversation. He always seemed to defend Daisy; she could do no wrong. When I learned that he had full access to her home and could come and go as he pleased, I lost it. Harris would never admit that he was sleeping with her, but when Junior was age 1 ½ years old, Daisy gave birth to Jamie.

At first, I was convinced it belonged to Lewis, this guy that Daisy was dating. Lewis seemed decent and liked Daisy and the kids, but at the end, she rejected him. Harris found everything wrong with the man and began making his presence known when he learned Lewis was not taking the rejection well.

After that situation, Harris and I started arguing about Daisy's life and not focusing on our own. Along with that came a lot of business plans that was making my purse light. Harris got into the housing business heavy, and it came with its ups and downs. We were struggling and I had to rely on my savings. In addition, taking care of two children was making it hard to maintain my clientele.

Learning that the housing business was rough, Harris got back into the streets heavy. I was happy that he could get things back on track, but I didn't agree with the illegal activity. With street life came street behavior and Harris was disappearing for days. I would have to search the city to find him sometimes and he very unpredictable. Trying to keep up with Harris was wearing me down; so, I invested that energy into Destiny and Junior and got back on my shit.

By the time Junior and Destiny was 8 years old, Harris stopped coming home all together. I found out he was living at the loft that I thought he sold. He showed up to everything for the kids. In fact, he became a better parent. However, he would never entertain any conversations about our relationship. He knew my image was important to me, so he would make sure that he only saw me in public places to avoid arguing.

I was so angry that our relationship failed. That's when I did the infamous 'Waiting to Exhale' move. You know when Angela Bassett burned her ex-husband's clothing up. I sat on my back patio and sipped wine while adding Harris's clothing to the fire pit.

Junior and Destiny called and told their daddy. He then called me and basically laughed at what I had done. He said burning his clothing only gave him a reason to shop and establish new shit, so I did not do anything special. He was right, but it helped to ease my pain that night.

As days went by, I fell into deep depression. Since he was on my cell plan, I spent time monitoring his text messages and looked at his call log daily. That's when I found out about Twyla. I remember blacking out and once I came back to reality, Harris was cleaning up the mess I made at home.

Once again, Junior and Destiny called their father because they were afraid. I was embarrassed at what I had done and stayed in my room for days. Then a week later, Harris contacted me for a sit down so that he could make peace with me. I appreciated him communicating with me about his feelings; but the rejection was still painful, and I would have to heal on my own.

Ever since that conversation, I have been taking it one day at a time. When Harris texted the information for the rehearsal dinner, we showed up. I sat and endured him giving another woman the love and affection that was intended for me. When it was over, I just exited the venue without saying goodbye to anyone and waited in the car for Destiny and Junior. It began to rain hard that night and I began to cry.

Suddenly, there was a tap on my window. It was Harris. I could barely wipe the tears from my face as he entered the passenger side of the car. Once inside, he asked me was I okay. I remember thinking how dumb his question was as I avoided eye contact. I asked him if he could drop the kids at the house later because I wasn't feeling well, before gesturing for him to get out of my car. He said okay and exited. I drove away.

I went home and cried in the shower before laying in my bed with a bottle of cabernet and listened to Mary J Blige sing my heart out for me. It was getting late, so I figured that Harris was keeping the kids at his place. So, I fell asleep.

In the middle of the night, I was awakened by soft kisses. When I opened my eyes, it was Harris. He made love to me while whispering "sorry" repeatedly. My heart was aching but his flesh against mine felt so good. When he finished, I laid in bed quietly and watched him dress before leaving. That was the last time I heard from him.

Junior had an allergic reaction last night and was rushed to the emergency room. I called, texted, and left a voicemail for Harris. No response yet. Something is wrong because Harris is always attentive to his children. Twyla claims that he is not answering her calls either which means he could have cold feet. Maybe I should call his homegirl, Rayvin, and see if she knows what is going on.

RAYVIN

Harris is the forbidden fruit in my life. My brothers were jealous of Harris and his family and used to tell me not to deal with them. I never got along with my brothers because they treated me like shit and my mother allowed them too, so of course, I did not listen to them.

Harris is good people in my eyes, besides the fact that he was a bonified womanizer. To spite my family, I allowed myself to be wide open with him and he became my best friend. We crossed the line and were intimate, but I don't regret that because we are bonded by things beyond sex.

I must admit that Harris can be addictive and dangerously manipulating. All the women are falling over each other, trying to get at him and have no idea how complex he is.

You see, Harris was not looking for a one-night stand to get his dick wet. He only dealt with women that served a purpose, and if your purpose was no longer valid in his life, then he was falling back for sure.

He is a selfish man. However, when it came to us, that

didn't matter because we have each other's back. Our loyalty is stronger than any one woman that he strings along.

I remember he would always say his number seven would be his wife. I laughed at his analogy, and now, I am here to witness that Twyla is his number seven and they are getting married. I am one of his best men.

Yes, you heard me correctly! Harris is 35 years old now and has only dealt with a couple of cougars during his teenage years. He does not count them along with the six women that he has strung along or damaged; plus, the one woman that has managed to take his complete heart. I include myself in the six women, but I don't feel strung along or damaged.

I met Harris when I was 16 years old. I was a rough tomboy that rip and ran with the boys all day long in the projects. I had a strict mother and could not go far. I had to be inside when the streetlight came on. My older brothers ran the streets, but they would never show me the way. Overtime, it was hard to fit in with the homies because I was starting to look too good, and everyone wanted to fuck. I went from the rough, messy hair having tomboy, to a beautiful chocolate goddess. Harris was the only one that didn't harass me sexually and that made us good friends.

Most of the time I could not go anywhere, so Harris would come and sit with me on the stairs everyday while he hustled. I was his lookout and decoy when the police came lurking. I didn't mind because it was the only excitement

I had in my life. My mother always took in other relatives who had a lot of children and I was stuck in the house babysitting.

My three older brothers, Ricky, Treavor, and Josh were not good role models. They ran the streets and were in and out of jail. They used to only come around to reprimand me when I was doing wrong; but it was really because they despised me dealing with Harris. They hated him because they wanted to carry his grandfather's, Alex, torch after he was murdered. But his son, Bennie, took over his father's business and left my brothers with nothing. So, they had to venture out the projects to make money.

I found it interesting that my brothers never expressed their feelings to Harris instead of talking to me. That was the influence Harris and his family had. Some people could not stand Bennie and Harris, but they always gave them their respect. Even Harris's mother ran the streets, but she got addicted to drugs for a while, and they sent her away to get sober. His younger sister, Shelby, was always fly and never lived in the projects with Harris and his mother. She lived with her father, who was a pastor.

I remember when Harris and I used to talk about everything on those stairs. We vented about our family issues and shared our dreams. He used to call me his Rapunzel because he would throw rocks at my window and I would throw his stash down in the middle of the night.

When I turned 17 years old, I was tired of being in the

house watching kids. Against my mother's wishes, I found me a job and focused on my grades during my junior year in high school. If I passed all my classes that year, then I would only have to go to school half a day my senior year; plus, graduate early in January instead of June. By that time, Harris was not tripping about the decoy thing because he was off to bigger and better things. His uncle moved the family out the hood. They were pushing weight to the projects and no longer needed to spend long nights selling pieces.

I am a living witness of Harris going from hundredaire to millionaire, and today he is well off, believe that. Harris and Bennie are the true definition of grit. They were born into that life and were true hustlers, starting from the bottom. If you were with them, then they had no problem sharing with you because they knew what the struggle felt like.

As time passed, I couldn't take it anymore. My mother and I had a big blowout and I ended up leaving in the middle of the night. Harris happened to be outside supplying someone and he gave me a ride to the hotel; after I declined the invite to his spot a few blocks away. I used my payroll check to pay for a hotel for a few months. But I was struggling, and working was taking me away from focusing on my grades.

One night, I was walking back to the hotel after spending my last dollar on some light groceries. Suddenly,

Harris emerged from one of the rooms and in an arrogant voice, told me I looked horrible. He questioned why I was still at the hotel he dropped me off at months ago and was concerned if I had become a junky.

His words were like sharp knives in my chest, but I held back emotions despite feeling fragile. Harris took a moment to observe my reaction before softening up. He then followed me to my room and tried to convince me to come move in his spot. After resisting for an hour, I gave in when he started taking my trash bags to his pick-up truck.

I don't even know what I was fighting about because Harris was a blessing. I was going to have to either check out that next morning, or give my virginity to the clerk, Wallace. He gave me that option when he noticed I was coming up short on my payments. And to be honest, I was desperate and was considering it. That night would have been the night if Harris did not show up.

I remember Wallace looking out the office door with hate in his eyes. I bet he probably had a room set up for us to fuck. We exited the hotel parking lot and road in silence. I felt a sense of relaxation, then my stomach began to rumble when we passed a couple food places. Harris must have heard it because he stopped at a small diner on the west side of town.

As we enjoyed our food, we caught up on each other lives over the past several months. He was doing well for himself and was saving up to invest in properties. He told me that the hood was not the same because everyone was moving out, including my mother. It saddened me to know that my mother would just pick up without worrying of whether her daughter was coming back. She knew I was friends with Harris so she could have sent a message. He observed my facial expression and told me he knew where she was and could take me there if I wanted to go. I declined the offer, but it meant a lot to me that he would keep up with my family for me.

After we ate, we headed to his place. It was a fourplex that he owned. His aunt, Racheal, lived in one of the bottom apartment units. He occupied both top levels, and of course, the other bottom level was used for his various business matters. Rachel was cool people. She looked out for Harris and his business matters in exchange for a place to call home. She used to run the streets with her father before he died, and after doing some time in prison, she just laid low. Rachel and I chilled every day, smoke, and ate because she could burn in the kitchen.

I continued to go to school and work while living with Harris. Every pay day, I handed him my money to later find back in my bedroom on the dresser. Not wanting to take a handout, I used the money to buy groceries and tried to race Harris to the utilities; just to feel like I was doing something besides keeping the apartment clean.

I was back on track, working hard, and keeping my grades up. I was able to graduate from high school early as planned. Harris and Rachel were in attendance, cheering me on as I walked across the stage. I did not bother to tell my mother or older brothers. I figured they never tried to come for me so what was the point in celebrating my achievement.

Harris did not hide the disgust he felt for my older brothers. He conducted business with them on a regular and they never even asked him if he had seen their sister or anything. I wonder if that is what made Harris look out for me more.

Shortly after my graduation, I enrolled in the local community college. I was going to show my family that they made a mistake by forgetting about me. Harris continued to look out for me, still never accepting any money from me. He said that a man takes care of his home and whomever is in it. Rachel was like a mother, always cooking for me and checking up on me when I was out.

I was happy and felt true love from family. That was important for me to thrive. I graduated from college with a Liberal Arts degree and had plans to attend a university to obtain my bachelor's degree in Forensic Science. I took a summer break that year, planning to live it up and celebrate my accomplishments before getting back to work. But in the summer of the year 2004, things would be unforgettable and change our lives forever.

People were always hating on Harris, but no one ever took things beyond arguments. That summer, someone started coming for Harris and Bennie hard and they could not figure out where the heat was coming from. He moved cautious all summer, hoping whomever he was into it with would not find the place he laid his head before he found them.

But being careful was not enough and trouble came to our doorstep on my 18th birthday. Harris and I were on the lower level at Rachel's. Of course, it was my first time drinking and Harris had me damn near gone off Hennessey. He said it was a required initiation for champions, and I was a champion. We took shots and watched Rachel dance; showing us how they used to do it back in the day. And just like that, bullets rained into the front window. We all hit the floor, and when the shooting stopped, I felt something wet on my right hand. I turned to find Rachel staring through me with dead eyes, she had a hole the size of a penny in her forehead.

I gasped; this was my first time seeing a dead body before it made it to the funeral home. It's an image that still haunts me.

Harris had tears flowing, but he had to keep his mind clear as possible as he stood from the floor. I knew the game from watching Harris operate, so I knew that we had some things to do fast before we could call for help. I stood up from the floor, grabbed the third glass of Hennessey, and washed it. Harris went to the other apartment and removed all illegal items, before going to the upper level and removing his safe and all valuable items.

We both operated in silence, stealing glances of Rachel's lifeless body on the floor. Harris kept asking me was I okay, and I kept nodding yes. I knew what my role would be without him even speaking. After he loaded everything into the pickup truck, he dashed down the back alley, leaving me alone with Rachel.

The silence in the apartment was loud. All the memories I shared with Rachel literally flashed before my eyes. I had to pull it together because the clock was ticking. I took in a deep breath, let my tears flow, then picked up the phone and dialed. When the operator answered, I screamed into the phone, "Oh God! Help my auntie has been shot! Please send help! Please!"

The police came and went through the apartment. It was no need to explain what happened based on all the bullet holes and shattered glass.

They did not conclude the crime scene until 7:00am. Once everyone was gone, I sat in silence alone, staring at the puddle of blood. I went into a trance and was awaken by the sound of hammering. Harris and Bennie were standing over me. I shook myself together, then went upstairs and packed what mattered to me. I hopped in the passenger side of the truck and we left the apartment. We arrived at a duplex across from Bennie's house.

Bennie had to start making funeral arrangements, so he left us at the new place. Harris and I sat in silence for a couple hours before he began showing his pain. I lost a lot of things that night, and Rachel's death took a part of both Harris and I. But it made our bond stronger. Rachel was his favorite and only aunt, and she was dear to me as well. I did not know how to console him, but I tried sitting alongside him and holding him. We cried off and on for several hours until Bennie returned.

The three of us sat, took shots of various clear and dark liquor, and tried to think about Rachel not being dead. I remember becoming numb and checking out. I woke up in a bed upstairs hours later. I looked around what would be my new bedroom. I got out of bed and found the bathroom, before rummaging through one of my bags to find a toothbrush and washcloth. I brushed my teeth and washed by face before going down to the lower apartment where Harris and Bennie had a full house.

Rachel's death brought a lot of people that were seldom seen. There was food and liquor throughout the day. After a while, everyone left, and I retreated to my bedroom. I fell into a deep sleep and the nightmares came. Images of Rachel's lifeless body consumed me. I awakened and found Harris was sitting on the bed beside me, crying. He laid next to me in the queen size bed. We laid facing each other, crying together until we both fell asleep.

The funeral service for Rachel was beautiful. Harris never left my side. Family and friends flooded me with hugs. For the first time, I saw my older brothers and they approached me displaying both confusion and hate in their eyes. I knew they probably wanted to rip my head off but would not dare display it in public. I didn't care how they felt because I was getting all the love I needed from Harris and his family. I was going to be okay.

After the repast, Harris and I returned to our new spot. Bennie instructed everyone to go to his house across the street and give us some space for the day. For the remainder of the evening, Harris and I sat and talked about Rachael. We were with her all the time and had a lot of funny memories. By the end of the night, we promised each other that we would avenge Rachael's death no matter what and at that moment, I became a gangster.

Harris and Bennie already had their ears to the streets. It did not take long to find out who was responsible for Racheal's death. I was ready and did not ask any questions. We made our move on a stormy Thursday night in August.

Harris, Bennie, Cameron, and I sat in the Chevy Caprice dressed in all black. Cameron was not feeling my presence, he was on some sexist shit that night. But I didn't let it take me off my game because Harris trained me well. Let me just say that Cameron has always been a winey, hating ass nigga. I often questioned why Harris trusted him because he had some sketchy ways.

But despite my lack of trust for Cameron, I had to give him credit because he was down for whatever, whenever.

When we saw some men entering the house, Cameron exited the car and made his way to the backyard. We waited for his signal and the three of us exited the car and jogged to the house. Bennie insisted that he kick in the door in honor of Rachel. We gave him that and entered guns blazing, not sparing a soul. Everything was in slow motion. It was like I could see every bullet flying, including the bullet I fired in the skull of my brother. Treavor. Guess you are wondering if I knew my brothers was my target. The answer is no.

With Treavor's blood on my hands, I was at a point of no return. We fled the scene in the pouring rain without a trace. There was no time to ponder on what just happened. We had to make our next move. There were more targets that were likely Ricky and Josh. Bennie and Cameron decided it would be best to do the second hit. So, they dropped Harris and I off at a night club to give us an alibi just in case this came back on us. Bennie knew the owner of the club and had our clothing in lockers of the employee lounge area in the back.

Harris and I dressed together, not caring that we were exposing our bodies to each other. As I stole a glimpse of his sexy body, I was feeling things that I never felt before. I stopped looking when I noticed him checking me out in the mirror. I slipped into my tight-fitting black dress and stilettos. We joined the party as if we had been there all night, making sure we were caught on a camera or two dancing together.

I felt fucked up at the beginning about my brother. But when I found out he knew I lived with Harris and shot the place up anyway, I got over the shit. That night, killing came natural to me. I knew Harris was concerned about me killing my flesh and blood. He did not waste any time bringing it up after we took a couple shots of Hornitos. But I ensured him that I was fine.

He warned me that it was likely my other two brothers would be dead as well. I looked Harris in the eyes and that's all he needed to see to know that my loyalty was to him.

Before the club wrapped up, we exited to beat the crowd. There was a black-on-black beamer waiting for us, compliments of Bennie. We spent the next few hours driving around the city in the rain before making it back to the spot around 6:00am.

I went straight to the bathroom to shower. The hot water poured all over my face and through my natural hair that had grown out thanks to the sew-ins. I just stood there thinking about my life and all the things that were happening.

Suddenly, my thoughts were disturbed by Harris, who had joined me in the shower. I did not object to his company as he grabbed the cloth and began washing my back. He was so gentle, making me feel so relaxed I almost lost my balance. He then took the washcloth between my legs and massaged me gently. I let out a low moan. I had never been touched like this before and it felt good. Harris grabbed a handful of my hair gently and pulled my face up to his. We kissed passionately for several minutes.

For the next half hour, we stayed in the shower kissing, touching, holding, and consoling each other. I could feel his manhood against me, and my love box was tingling, wanting him inside of me. When I felt his finger trying to penetrate me, I pushed him back and warned him that I was a virgin. He looked at me for several seconds, I could tell he did not believe what he was hearing and maybe he was hoping that I would say sike or something.

When I didn't say anything, he gave me another kiss, then reached behind me. He turned off the shower and exited the bathroom. I stood in the shower embarrassed, thinking how I must have been the only 18-year-old virgin in the world.

Several minutes later, he returned, finding me in the same exact spot with my hands buried in my face. He grabbed one of my hands, leading my butt naked, wet body out of my bathroom.

He took me to his bedroom and into his private bathroom. He had the hot tub going. I gave him a questioning look as I stepped into the hot tub, submerging myself into the warm water. Harris put on some jazz before joining me. I allowed the soft music to take me away while Harris planted soft kisses on me. He made his way down to my navel, before straddling my legs around his neck. I used my arms to hold my upper body above the water while Harris let his tongue do the talking.

I must of went to heaven and back because his tongue

felt amazing. I could not believe I was holding out and cheating myself out of this. I remember receiving several offers from men to just suck my pussy and I declined. But now that I think about it, they probably would not have done it like Harris.

I must have had at least twenty orgasms within that hour, his tongue was relentless. I was so exhausted from the orgasms that he picked me up and took me to his bed. He dried me off and oiled my body with baby oil. We fell asleep naked, holding each other. While I slept, I dreamed of Rachel alive and smiling at me.

Hours later, I was awakened by soft kisses from Harris. My pussy was still throbbing from his tongue and was ready to go. He whispered in a low seductive voice, "Are you ready to go all the way?" I answered, "Yes." He took my virginity gently that afternoon.

He was packing and it took me a week to get used to him. From that point forward, we were fucking like rabbits while running the streets like pit bulls. Harris taught me everything I know in the bedroom. We watched pornos, role played, and had random sex in the craziest places.

As time passed, we were more money motivated and the flame that sparked soon began to dampen. We had chemistry and I was in love with him because he was my first and only. But I knew what type of man Harris was, and I backed away to protect my heart and our friendship.

I kept quiet and endured his relationships with Toni, May, Daisy, Tameka, and Loretta.

From my view, all these bitches had unique issues. The only two that loved him like I did was Daisy and Tameka. All the other bitches were looking for a nigga to save them, in some type of way. Especially that whore, Loretta. I swear I am going to put a bullet in her head when I get the chance to.

Harris is in love with this chick named Twyla. She seems cool, and Harris has completely changed. A lot of the street shit has been left in my hands and I am stuck working with Cameron's ass.

I heard that Harris has not checked in with his children or been heard from and that is a definite red flag. I check his secret safe daily and the amount is still the same. Trust and believe Harris is not leaving no money behind. So, I am hitting the streets hard to find him and paying a visit to Daisy, Tameka, May, Toni, Loretta, and Twyla whether they like it or not.

DAISY

I remember when I first met Harris in grade school. He had a crush on me and would harass me all the time. I would act like I didn't care about his advances, but I looked forward to them every day. Harris was my first love and we were friends. I remember watching him go from a dusty, hard head boy to a man, running the streets and taking care of his family.

Harris and I were madly in love, but our strong personalities clashed a lot. We struggled with our young love until age 21 when our twin daughters, Clarise and Daisha, were born. Our relationship was dysfunctional. He had a couple ongoing affairs with a couple older women who kissed and never told. At the beginning, it was hard to know exactly what was going on. But things came to the light when this older woman everyone called Cookie started tripping. One night, she was waiting outside my apartment. She said that she and Harris were in love and he was going to marry her, but she didn't even have on an engagement ring.

When Harris found out, he was pissed. He brought me a gun and took me to the shooting range every week. After that, I felt it was best to back up from him and focus on our daughters. I figured that once we matured, we could try later. But Harris started pursuing relationships with other women.

I tried to keep a straight face and move on, but it was hard to get over him. Finally, I met Lewis. That seemed promising, then Harris came along and ran him the fuck off. I was pissed! He had the guy so scared that he would not even answer my calls. I knew May was jealous of Harris and I. She probably thinks I intentionally sabotaged their relationship. But that was not the case at all. After that, I was fed up with Harris controlling my life. I began to make plans to move out of state so that I could start a new life without his interference. I was not going to keep him away from his daughters, so I went to Bennie and talked to him about my plans. I was tired of looking at Harris toggle all these different women. During that time, it was Toni, May, Rayvin, and Tameka.

Toni was supposed to be a crack head that cooked his dope at his spot, but then Destiny was born. May was this conceded bitch that was not even Harris's type. She had his son and Destiny moved in with her. I remember coming to the hospital and supporting Tameka when she lost Majestic. I was just waiting for Rayvin to come up pregnant, but she was way too gangster for that, I guess. I really think she is a lesbian.

Bennie told me that he would look out for me no matter

what decision I made because I was family. That's one thing I loved about Harris's family, they were real and they looked out for each other. Hell, he had Tameka living in his house and if I needed a place to stay he probably would have let me stay there too.

After receiving my blessing from Bennie, I proceeded to make plans to move to Atlanta. I terminated my lease and packed all my shit. Of course, Bennie told Harris and I ignored his calls all that week. I knew he would try and talk me out of it. I decided to allow the girls to stay with Bennie while I went down and got settled.

The night before the flight, I checked into a hotel by the airport so that Harris would not find me. Unknowing to me, the entire time he was following me. While I slept, Harris talked the hotel manager into giving him a key to my room.

Well, I didn't end up catching that flight, and nine months later I was in the hospital pushing out our daughter, Jamie. Bennie brought his comical ass up to the hospital teasing me. He told me to name my baby Georgia. So, of course, per his request, my baby's full name is Jamie Georgia Marie Grimes.

The new baby did not revive our relationship. But we were still great friends and co-parent well with our daughters. Even though I knew he had bitches in the walls, Harris still made me happy and kept me satisfied sexually. No dick has out done him yet and he kept me full of it. I always wondered why our chemistry was so loud, but we could not function in a relationship.

But our situation-ship was working, and the girls were happy. So, I endured Harris's rapture and tolerated Toni, May, Tameka, Rayvin, and then, here came Loretta's crazy ass. I thought that Toni was the worst baby momma, but Loretta took the cake. When you looked up the word crazy in the dictionary, that bitch picture should be there. I had to question Harris when he made a baby with Loretta. He admitted that it was only a sex thing and he got caught slipping.

As usual, I tried to support him and help with his new deadbeat baby momma. Loretta was so busy trying to manipulate Harris, that she didn't even pay attention to what was happening. Harris hired a lawyer, took Loretta's ass to court, and got full custody of Karris. I will tell you this! Harris would have to kill me before he could just take my daughters away from me!

It was crazy watching the epic failure of the gold digger Loretta. She thought she was about to snatch a nigga that paid bills and ended up back in the projects at her mother's place with that bucket he bought her. Let me stop because God don't like ugly. But I knew from the day I talked to Loretta on that patio that she was on some gold-digging shit. One thing I know, is that Harris is very selective with the type of women he chooses. I can say in confidence that he is probably the only man I know with womanizing tendencies and a low body count.

However, this chick Twyla just came out of nowhere and has the man in Harris that I have been waiting for her. They have a wedding coming up in a few days. Today everyone has been looking for him. I think he has cold feet. Junior had an allergic reaction, and he did not surface for that; so, something must be wrong. I have called all the hospitals and jails in the Kansas City area with no luck.

TWYLA

Harris was the guy that all the women wanted, including me, even though he was ten years older that I. I was the quiet, good girl in the projects. My mother never allowed me to socialize with the kids in the neighborhood, so I spent a lot of time in school, at my grandparent's church, or in my bedroom reading.

I remember sitting in my bedroom window for hours, looking outside at all the action going on in "Parker Square". I used to watch Harris all the time hustling outside. Over time, the more money he made, the less I saw him. My mother, Lynetta, better known as Cookie, started letting me on the porch. That's how I met Cameron, Harris's best friend.

Cameron was always lurking in the hood all hours of the day and night. That was fine with me because I had someone to talk to when I was on the porch or in my bedroom window. One day, my mother caught me talking to Cameron. I thought I would be in trouble and lose my porch privilege, but to my surprise, she didn't trip. I learned later why.

One stormy night when I woke up to go get a glass of water, I thought I was in a dream. I saw my mother on her knees in the middle of the living room, giving Harris head. I never seen my mother even take a drink of alcohol before, so it mortified me. I returned to my bedroom quietly and made myself go back to sleep.

Seeing the sexual acts at a young age opened an erotic door. My next few nights consisted of sneaking and watching my mother and Harris. He would come at 3:00am almost every night and he would stay until sunrise.

When I saw Cameron again, I questioned whether he knew about it. I could tell by the shocked expression on his face that it was news to him. I remember Cameron saying that my mother was the pretties most stuck-up woman in the hood and he could not believe she was a cougar. From that day moving forward, Cameron and I grew closer. I started sneaking him through my bedroom window. While my mother was downstairs being a super freak, Cameron was climbing through my window, turning me into a woman. I enjoyed every moment of being taken advantage of. Cameron was doing things to me that I didn't know even exist. I know what you are thinking, and yes, you are right. Cameron was committing statutory rape. I was only 12 years old when he started climbing through my window.

Months went by and my mother and I continued to hide our secrets from each other. But that all changed when Harris got into her head and our place became the chill spot for him and Cameron. When Harris was over, my mother would not allow me to come downstairs. When they ran arrands, she would let Cameron stay. While they were gone, you already know what was going on between Cameron and me.

Soon, the dynamics of our house started to change. My mother was no longer making me go to church with my grandparents and she started drinking. I expressed my concern to Cameron. He encouraged me to go with the flow and that he would handle it. At that point, we were in love and had plans on running away together when I was 18 years old.

Then, things turned for the worse. Harris began to lose interest for my mother. He did what everyone man would do and that was divide and conquered. My mother was a conquest for Harris. She was the "Ms. Jackson" of the hood and every man had only dreamed of being with her. She was youthful for her age, with her smooth milk high yellow skin, and natural reddish-brown hair. She was a redbone who kept her hair right and body tight. She didn't hang in the hood and was only seen coming and going. I was the chocolate version of my mother, gaining my dark complexion from my father who was African. No one ever saw me, but Cameron. He said it was better that way because he did not have time to shoot a nigga over me.

As weeks passed, the less that Harris came around, the crazier my mother was. Cameron told me that she was stalking Harris. She found his spots and was popping up. The freaky nights in the bedroom turned into cold lonely nights of tears for my mother. She started having these episodes and Cameron would have to convince Harris to come put the fires out. Harris would come argue, have sex with her, and argue more when it was time for him to go. I knew he had lost all respect for my mother when the other dudes in the neighborhood started trying to pursue her.

Then, mother lost her job, turned into a hood rat, then the door was revolving. When she began doing drugs to numb the pain, when I was 13, she sent me away to live with my grandparents.

I would sneak Cameron into my grandparent's house while they slept. He would give me updates on my mother. He said he was basically selling drugs out of her apartment and taking care of the bills. He told me to never come there because I would not be able to handle what my mother had become. He told me that Harris was not even coming around to put the fires out anymore.

One Sunday, when I road with my grandparents, I insisted on stopping by to drop my mother off some food to eat. When we parked in front of the apartment, there were niggas hanging out on the porch. The blinds were all torn up on every window, and it was trash scattered all over. Cameron stood on the sidewalk away from the apartment watching. He looked at me in the back seat and shook his head.

She would not let my grandfather inside, but when she came ono the front porch I almost screamed. My mother looked horrible. She was skinny and her long hair was broken off bad. My grandfather prayed with my mother on that porch and tried to convince her to just get in the car and leave all of this.

Then, the words that I would never forget came out of my mother's mouth as I sat with the back window down, listening. She said she could not leave because Harris would not be able to find her. I looked over at Cameron who mouthed the words, "I am sorry."

When we drove away, leaving my mother, I had a newfound hate for Harris that I never had for anyone or anything in the world. That was the last time I saw my mother alive. One night I was missing my mother and Cameron was not answering my calls or text. So, I took a drastic move and stole my grandmother's car. I drove straight to her apartment.

When I arrived, there was no niggas hanging out like before. The door was unlocked, so I walked in and went straight to my mother's bedroom. I opened the door, and that's when I made the tragic discovery.

My mother laid in bed, dead. She had taken some pills and killed herself. She wrote a suicide note and it was all about Harris and how he had rejected her; that she could not live without him. I folded the note and put it in my pocket before calling the paramedics.

Later, I showed Cameron the letter and we were the only two that knew about it. Harris didn't come to my mother's funeral! So, I copied the letter and mailed it to his Uncle Bennie's house so he could know that he was the reason my mother died. Cameron said Harris read the note and was really messed up. Out of guilt, Harris upgraded my mother's headstone.

I demanded my grandparents to send me to a boarding school away from Kansas City for a while. I spent my days focusing on myself and my future. My grandparents and Cameron were my support system through it all. I returned to Kansas City on my mother's 10-year anniversary and ran into Harris at Speedy's liquor store. During that time, I was 23 years old and he was flirting with me. I was so angry inside because he had no idea who I was. It infuriated me that Harris spent so much time in our home and never took the time to know her precious child. That validated my mother didn't mean a thing to him. I remember crying in Cameron's arms that night. But over time, I made so much progress in healing.

Seeing Harris happy and moving on with his life took me back to day one. My mother was six feet under in a box because she fell in love with a little boy that wanted nothing more but to have sex with her.

I missed my mother, and someone was going to pay. So, when Cameron expressed how he and Harris's friendship was on the rocks, I took the opportunity to formulate a plan that would get retribution for the both of us. The plan I had would get Cameron the money and power he deserved, and the revenge I needed for my mother's death.

It took me months to convince Cameron. He didn't like the idea of his woman sleeping with another man. But his greed wanted to walk in Harris's shoes, so he would sacrifice. I started making my move, getting out more, exposing myself to places where I would run into Harris. And just like bate, he took it. To my surprise, he fell in love with me fast.

Cameron hated it. But I kept him at bey, reminding him of the prize at the end. I was shocked that within a year, I had a ring on my finger and a couple of his children were coming around often. I won't lie, I was falling a little bit, and my love for Cameron was being buried deeper into our lies and deceit. Harris had serious swag and was giving me the business in the bedroom. I had to use my mother's suicide to take me out of the clouds more often. I wasn't ready to stop, so I convinced Cameron that if I married Harris, I could gain more access to both his legal and illegal money.

Cameron was not going for that and was ready to make his move once I found out all the information he needed. We were down to days before the wedding and Cameron said there was no more time to waste. I think he sensed that I was falling for Harris.

So, I stole some morphine after I clocked out at the hospital and headed home where Harris awaited like a puppy dog every night. Cameron was parked outside, letting me know it was going down or he was blowing up the whole thing.

I was a little down that night because, in a way, I was enjoying co-habituating with Harris. He knew how to treat a woman and we lived so lavish. That night, he made my favorite meal and ran my bath. We were planning for a baby, but I knew that was not happening because I was taking birth control. But I was enjoying the efforts. It was something about a man making love to you while whispering in your ear that he wanted you to have his baby. After dinner and the soaking in the tub, I added some morphine to the wine and stood over Harris as he slipped peacefully away.

When he was out, I unlocked the front door for Cameron. We put Harris in the trunk of his own car that was parked inside the garage. I sent deceptive text messages to Harris phone, inquiring when he was coming home.

Everyone thought Harris had cold feet, until a couple of days after the wedding. Cassandra, Shelby, and Bennie were at my doorstep daily and we filed a police report. Nervous Cameron staged a break in and stole the safe that contained the three million dollars that Harris earned through blood and sweat.

I won't lie, I am a bit paranoid. I heard Harris had a lot of heavy hitters on his team like Rayvin and Bennie. I watch the news daily and keep my ears to the street. But I think we did a wonderful job covering things up. The only thing I regret was not revealing to Harris why this happened to him. Cameron wanted to get things over with. I think he was more afraid of Harris than anyone. I hope Harris is looking up from the deep pits of hell watching me tell this story. Cameron and I plan to play it cool and slip out of the country very soon and live happily ever after.

HARRIS: NIGHT BEFORE THE WEDDING

The last thing I remember seeing was Twyla handing me a glass of wine. I am normally not a wine drinker, but tonight was special. Note to self, "Do not drink wine again." But that would be the least of my worries because I cannot open my eyes or move. I am in some type of paralyzed state. Only my hearing and thoughts seem normal. The familiar sound around me is my hemi engine roaring, so I must be inside my car. However, I am confused on what is going on. Did someone bust into the house? Is Twyla okay?

Wait! I hear a familiar ring tone. That's Cameron's phone and he is answering it. From the sound of the conversation, whomever he is talking too is a female because he keeps saying, "Baby, it is going to be okay just follow me."

Now at this point, I know that something happened to me and that Twyla is following Cameron. Maybe we are going to the hospital. But why is Twyla and Cameron not riding together. What happened to me?

The car has stopped, and Cameron just turned the engine off. He has exited the car and it sounds like he is walking on gravel or something. I hear another car and the squeaking sound reminds me of Cameron's old-school Chevy. I hear more footsteps. Now, complete silence. At this point, I am sure I am not at a hospital.

I hear Twyla's voice. She just said that she wishes she would have told me who she was before I died. Cameron is saying not to worry because Twyla finally has her revenge and they can move on with their lives.

What the fuck! I know this must be a nightmare! My best friend and the love of my life conspired to kill me, and I am dead. Well, that explains the paralyses and why I can only hear, because I am dying.

Wait, Twyla is talking again. She said that she hopes that her mother is waiting for me in the afterlife. Why would her mother be waiting for me? She makes it sound as if her mother is upset with me.

Cameron is saying that Twyla's mother committed suicide and will be waiting for me in hell. Twyla is offended by his statement. Twyla never told me that her mother committed suicide, and what would any of this have to do with me. Wait! The only person I know that killed themselves was Cookie.

Fuck! Twyla is Cookie's daughter for sure. I never really paid her any attention when I came through. She was supposed to be in her bedroom asleep.

I remember Cameron revealing to me that he crept up there a couple times and was breaking her in. I told him to stop that shit before he caught a case.

Damn, Cookie! I have never forgot about what happened. She just got lost in her feelings and spiraled out of control. I was so young at that time and didn't really understand the damage I was doing.

Before things got bad, Cookie was cool peoples. She stayed to herself and was focused. Every nigga in the hood wanted Cookie; she was like a dream that would never come true. We used to call her Ms. Jackson. I never thought I would ever have a chance with her. Until one night, I was hanging out and hustling. The cops came through and harassed me. Cookie watched them take turns beating me with the pitons, before taking my money and leaving me on the curve bloody.

When they were gone, Cookie came to my aid and took me inside and she cleaned my wounds. Man, I still remember her scent that night. She smelled so fresh it reminded me of peaches. I thanked God for the nuisance cop before I took a chance and made a move. Cookie's white house coat was coming undone a bit, exposing just the inner rim of one of her breasts. I knew that she knew her shit was open. She was pressed against me while dabbing my lip with a damp towel. I know she felt that rock hard 20-year-old dick rising through my jeans. I was ready to taste what was under that robe.

Just like my mother's best friend taught me, I eased my hands under her robe and touched her gently. Her skin was so soft and smooth like butter. My dick was precumming just feeling her body. Cookie didn't resist me and she let her robe fall to the floor. I took time to admire her beautiful body; she had a small scar below her naval that I later learned was from a tuba ligation. She was perfect and giving the girls my age a run for their money.

I wrapped my mouth around one of her breast and sucked softy. I could feel her body going limp; she began to moan softly, and I took that invite to ease between her legs. Her wetness let me know she wanted this more than me. So, with one index finger, I went in and out slowly while continuing to savor her breast in my mouth. Cookie opened my jeans and released my manhood. She straddled me on the toilet and road me until I came. It was the best and from that point moving forward, I was coming through damn near every night, fucking the shit out of her.

Over time, feelings started to develop, and Cookie wanted a relationship. I was young and was still trying with Daisy, who was pregnant with twins. Cookie was like 36 years old and I really though she just wanted to play with some young dick. Her tubes were tied, and I wanted children, how far were we really going to go?

I admit I was addicted to the sex, but that relationship shit was not happening. When I broke things off, Cookie became jealous, possessive, and was popping up at my spots.

She was starting fights with women that she seen coming in and out. Then, Cameron started hustling out of her spot and would beg me to come down when she was tripping out so that she would not put him out.

Just to help him out, I would come calm her down, have sex with her, sing sweet nothings in her ear, then go home once she fell into a deep sleep. Soon, I learned from Cameron that she was on drugs heavy and lost her job. I witnessed her beauty wither into an empty shell. Cookie was lost and I didn't know what to do about it, so I would avoid the situation.

She would write me long ass letters and mail them to my uncle Bennie's. I read every letter and I did nothing about this woman falling apart. I was young and didn't know how to handle it, so I just turned the other cheek and hoped she would get over it.

When Cameron gave me the news that Cookie committed suicide, I damn near passed out. I felt so fucked up, I didn't even go to the funeral. Then, one day I received another letter in the mailed and it had Cookie's name on it. It spooked me because she was dead. It was the suicide letter. She took her life because she could not have me, and I have to live with knowing that for the rest of my life. Out of guilt, I upgraded her head stone and would visit to keep the flowers fresh.

Cookie's death changed how I dealt with women. I no longer wanted to just fuck because a woman was sexy or willing to give it up. We had to have some type of connection beyond the bedroom. During that time in my life, I figured that if I gave a woman something emotionally valuable, then once we went our separate ways, they were not likely to spiral out of control like Cookie did. It may sound crazy, but I was afraid to break up with another chick; so, I ended up with six of them.

I know you are saying maybe I just should just not fuck with anyone until I know for sure. But you tell my dick that and see the response you receive. My method was going well until the day I met Twyla. She made me mature and I realized that a man would do right for who he really wants. I was ready to share everything with her.

Now, I am in this fucked up situation! And my own homie, my brother is a part of the madness. I can't really be mad at Twyla though because it probably devastated her to watch her mother fall apart like that, so I can respect the revenge. But Cameron, I can never forgive him. It's time to look in the mirror and take responsibility. I have been a womanizer for years and women have cried oceans of tears and fallen because of me. I have been selfish and now it has cost me my life.

Daisy was my childhood sweetheart. I loved her like family but didn't want her to ever love any other man like she loved me. So, I kept her in lieu, but didn't want to commit to her.

Tameka was alone and when she lost Majestic, I was

determined to define the laws of nature to make her a mother to fix her.

Rayvin was a rider. I loved her loyalty and ambition. She loved everything I loved and would risk her life for me. I knew Trevor was in that house that night when I took her, but at that time, I didn't care because he shot into a place where he knew his sister lived.

Loretta, that chick was crazy. I never loved her. I got trapped in the lust of the situation and ended up with a beautiful daughter. I didn't feel she deserved to be a mother, so I took Karris and gave her to Tameka.

I loved May's independence and ambition. She was about money like me, and I saw us making millions together. But to be honest, she intimidated me because she was too independent.

And Toni, I saved her from abuse only to abuse her myself. She saw the ugliest side of me and I used her destitute situation to string her alone. When she told me she was pregnant, I made her have the baby. She didn't want children because she knew she was fucked up, but I didn't care about her feelings.

Twyla was my Karma for Cookie and all the woman that I used and abused all these years. All I can do is accept my fate and hope that God forgives me.

Now, I can hear the trunk opening. It sounds like I am being dragged and was tossed into a hole. Damn! No bullet in the head to finish me off. I can hear the dirt being tossed on me. Damn, being buried alive was my worst fear. I can feel my chest tight now and my ears are starting to ring, maybe this is officially the end.

ONE WEEK LATER

I just opened my eyes and can see the sun shining. Thank God for forgiving a nigga and letting me into heaven! This room reminds me of one of Bennie's bedrooms, all decked out and shit.

Harris sat up on the bed, relieved that he could see and move on his own. He stood, walked over to the window, and looked out onto the ocean. Suddenly, he heard footsteps. Harris turned, anticipating who would enter the room.

When the older Hispanic woman entered, Harris sighed in relief.

The woman smiled before speaking. "I am glad you are awake, young man. We rescued you just in time," finished the woman. She began making up the bed Harris was laying in.

Harris looked around before questioning, "Is this heaven?"

The woman laughed before responding. "Thanks for the compliment, but you are not in heaven. You are very much alive and well. My husband and I have a private airport in Kansas City. We saw two people burying you by the river. We waited until they left, dug you up, and brought you to our home in Miami." The woman joined Harris at the window before continuing. "We have not notified any authorities because, based on my husband's line of work, we knew that for two people to bury you alive it must be something illegal going on. I'm just glad that we were there."

Harris looked out the window and continued to admire the ocean. He was going to contact Bennie and Rayvin and get back to Kansas City.

The End.

ABOUT THE AUTHOR

Rosa James is a newly published author born and raised in Kansas City, Missouri. Biologically she is the oldest of six children. At age 11 she and her brothers and sisters were placed into foster care. By age 14 she and her siblings were adopted by the same family, and Rosa became the middle child of 18 children. Rosa recognized her passion for writing at an early age and has always dreamed of publishing a book.

Becoming a single parent at age 18, Rosa was determined to beat the odds and raise her four children. She continued her education and obtained a Bachelor's in Human Service Management in the year 2012, followed by a Master's in General Psychology in 2015.

Rosa published her first book "Loyal Snakes" in January 2021.

PASSION2RIGHT.COM

Lightning Source UK Ltd.
Milton Keynes UK
UKHW010923021121
393249UK00001B/289